BONES
and the MATH TEST Mystery

A Puffin Easy-to-Read

BY DAVID A. ADLER

ILLUSTRATED BY BARBARA JOHANSEN NEWMAN

PUFFIN BOOKS
An Imprint of Penguin Group (USA) Inc.

For Eve's granddaughter, Sophie Noa—D.A.

For my parents, for just being here —B.J.N.

PUFFIN BOOKS
Published by the Penguin Group
Penguin Young Readers Group, 345 Hudson Street, New York, New York 10014, U.S.A.
Penguin Group (Canada), 90 Eglinton Avenue East, Suite 700, Toronto, Ontario, Canada M4P 2Y3
(a division of Pearson Penguin Canada Inc.)
Penguin Books Ltd, 80 Strand, London WC2R 0RL, England
Penguin Ireland, 25 St Stephen's Green, Dublin 2, Ireland (a division of Penguin Books Ltd)
Penguin Group (Australia), 250 Camberwell Road, Camberwell, Victoria 3124, Australia
(a division of Pearson Australia Group Pty Ltd)
Penguin Books India Pvt Ltd, 11 Community Centre, Panchsheel Park, New Delhi - 110 017, India
Penguin Group (NZ), 67 Apollo Drive, Rosedale, North Shore 0632, New Zealand
(a division of Pearson New Zealand Ltd.)
Penguin Books (South Africa) (Pty) Ltd, 24 Sturdee Avenue,
Rosebank, Johannesburg 2196, South Africa

Registered Offices: Penguin Books Ltd, 80 Strand, London WC2R 0RL, England

First published in the United States of America by Viking,
a division of Penguin Young Readers Group, 2008
Published by Puffin Books, a division of Penguin Young Readers Group, 2010

3 5 7 9 10 8 6 4

Text copyright © David A. Adler, 2008
Illustrations copyright © Barbara Johansen Newman, 2008
All rights reserved

THE LIBRARY OF CONGRESS HAS CATALOGED THE VIKING EDITION AS FOLLOWS:
Adler, David A.
Bones and the math test mystery / by David A. Adler ; illustrated by Barbara Johansen Newman.
p. cm. — (Viking easy-to-read)
Summary: Detective Jeffrey Bones hates taking math tests,
especially one he has forgotten to study for, so when his test paper goes missing he must make
a choice—retake the test and try to do better, or find the missing paper.
ISBN: 978-0-670-06262-1 (hc)
[1. Examinations—Fiction. 2. Mathematics—Fiction.
3. Lost and found possessions—Fiction. 4. Schools—Fiction. 5. Mystery and detective stories.]
I. Newman, Barbara Johansen, ill. II. Title.
PZ7.A2615Bom 2008 E—dc22 2007017901

Puffin Books ISBN 978-0-14-241519-1
Puffin® and Easy-to-Read® are registered trademarks of Penguin Group (USA), Inc.
Manufactured in China

-CONTENTS-

1. An Upside-Down Candy Cane

My Name is Bones,

Jeffrey Bones.

I am a detective.

I solve mysteries.

I also go to school.

My teacher is Mr. Gale.

He is very smart.

He loves to read.

He can read really big words.

But sometimes he loses things.

Well, lots of times he loses things.

This morning he lost his eyeglasses.

"Look up," I said.

He looked at the ceiling.

"No," I told him.

"Look on your head."

"How could I do that?" he asked.

I left my seat

and stood on his chair.

I took his eyeglasses off his head.

"Thank you," Mr. Gale said.

My work the day Mr. Gale

lost his eyeglasses

was writing the letter J.

That's my letter.

It starts my name, Jeffrey.

Capital J is fun to write.

It's like an upside-down candy cane

with a flat hat.

I wrote lots of Js,

big Js and small Js.

Then Mr. Gale said,

"Put your Js away.

It's time for a math test."

"Oh, no," I said.

I like writing Js.

I don't like doing math.

2. I Forget Things

Mr. Gale loses things.

I forget things.

I forgot that Mr. Gale told us

we would have a math test.

He told us to study adding facts.

I forgot to study.

"I hate math tests," I said.

"Not me," one girl said.

"I love math tests."

She always says, "Not me."

Her name is Amy.

But lots of people call her

"Not-Me Amy."

Mr. Gale gave me a test.

The page was filled with numbers.

Add this to that. Add that to this.

Mr. Gale sat behind his desk

and opened a newspaper.

It's not fair! I thought.

He gets to do what he wants,

and I have to do math.

I turned and looked

at my detective bag.

That bag is filled with things

to help me solve mysteries,

but not number mysteries.

I looked at my test paper.

I did not want to add all those numbers.

Mr. Gale looked up from his newspaper.

"Your time is almost up," he said.

I hurried.

Mr. Gale dropped his newspaper

on his desk.

He stood and said,

"Please, bring me your papers."

I was not done.

I wrote lots of numbers,

just any numbers, on my paper.

I was the last one to finish.

I dropped my test on Mr. Gale's desk.

"Line up for lunch," Mr. Gale said.

I went to lunch.

"I wish we didn't have to learn

about numbers," I said at lunch.

"Not me," someone said,

and you know who said it.

It was Not-Me Amy.

After lunch Mr. Gale smiled.

"You all did very well on your tests.

"But Jeffrey," he asked. "Where is yours?"

"I put it on your desk," I said.

"But I don't have it," Mr. Gale told me.

Mr. Gale gave out the papers.

He gave a paper to everyone but me.

"Wow!" Not-Me Amy said.

"I got every answer right."

"So what," I said.

"Maybe you can add,

but I can solve mysteries."

"Can you?" Not-Me Amy asked.

"Then where is your test paper?

Can you solve that mystery?"

3. Sticky Turkeys

"Soon it will be Thanksgiving,"

Mr. Gale said.

"Today we'll make Thanksgiving cards.

You can give one to your parents.

You can give some to your friends."

Mr. Gale gave everyone

red, green, and yellow

blank papers. Everyone but me.

He also gave everyone but me paste

and turkey papers—

you know, papers with pictures of turkeys.

"Cut out the turkeys," Mr. Gale said.

"Paste them on the blank papers

and make cards."

Then Mr. Gale came to my desk.

"While they make cards," he said,

"you have to take the math test."

"Again?" I asked.

"Yes, again," Mr. Gale said.

"I need to know if you can add."

I looked at all those numbers.

I didn't want to add them again.

"Mr. Gale," I said.

"I'll find my math test.

I'll find the one I put on your desk."

I took my detective bag and

opened it.

I looked for something

to help me find my math test.

All I found was a fake beard,

detective powder,

and a magnifying glass.

"This stuff won't help," I said.

"Shh," Not-Me Amy told me.

"I'm sticking turkeys to my cards."

I looked at Not-Me Amy.

I looked at her sticky turkeys.

"That's it!" I said.

"I did it again.

I solved the mystery.

I know where to find my math test."

4. But I'm a Detective!

"Hey, Mr. Gale," I called.

"I think I know where

to find my math test."

Mr. Gale came to my desk.

He looked at my paper.

Mr. Gale said,

"You haven't done even one problem."

"But," I said, "I think I know where

to find my math test,

the one I put on your desk.

The sticky turkeys

gave me the answer.

I think my test got stuck

behind another test."

"Please," Mr. Gale told the class,

"take out your math tests.

See if Jeffrey's test is stuck to yours."

All the students took out their tests.

Not-Me Amy held up her paper.

"It's not stuck to mine," she said.

Mr. Gale had written *Excellent!*

on the top of her paper.

"It's not stuck to mine,"

lots of children called out.

I looked at their papers, too.

Mr. Gale had written *Excellent!*

on all their papers.

"Well," Mr. Gale said.

"We didn't find your test.

Now, please do the math problems."

But I'm a detective, I thought.

I know I put my test on

Mr. Gale's desk.

But where was it?

I had to solve this mystery!

I looked at Mr. Gale.

First he helped children

with their cards.

Then he sat behind his desk

and read a book.

I told you.

He loves to read.

He stopped reading.

He put a bookmark in his book.

He closed his book.

I looked at Mr. Gale.

I looked at his desk.

"That's it!" I said.

"Now I'm sure I solved

this mystery.

Now I know where

to find my test."

5. I Solved the Mystery

I went to Mr. Gale.

"Jeffrey," he asked.

"Have you finished your math test?"

"No," I told him.

"But I think I know where to find

the one I put on your desk.

Your bookmark helped me solve the mystery."

"It did?" Mr. Gale asked.

"Yes," I said. "I think my test

is your newspaper mark."

"My newspaper mark?"

Mr. Gale asked.

"Yes," I said.

"You told me to put my test

on your desk.

"I did.

But your open newspaper

was on your desk, too.

I think I put it on your newspaper.

Later you closed your newspaper.

If I open your newspaper

to the page you were reading,

I think I'll find my test."

Mr. Gale said,

"I was reading page eighteen.

"I was reading about

a new book."

I opened the newspaper to page 18.

There it was, my test.

"Hey, I found it," I said.

"I solved the mystery."

I was about to give it to Mr. Gale.

But then I looked at the test paper.

Hey, I thought,

4 + 5 is not 327!

6 + 2 is not 288!

All these answers are wrong!

"Mr. Gale," I said.

"Lots of my answers are wrong.

May I take the test again?"

"Yes," he said.

I folded the test

with all the wrong answers.

I put it in my pocket.

I went to my desk

and did all the problems again.

This time,

I didn't hurry.

I tried to get the right answers.

I wanted Mr. Gale to write *Excellent!*

on my paper, too.